POCKET PUZZLES

Scholastic Inc.

ISBN 978-1-338-74084-4

10 9 8 7 6 5 4 3 2 1   21 22 23 24 25

Printed in China
First printing 2021

Cover design by Cheung Tai
Interior design by Kay Petronio

WELCOME, TRAINERS!

This book is full of fun Pokémon puzzles and activities to bend your brain and test your knowledge. Grab a pen or pencil and join your favorite Pokémon pals! Answers are at the back of the book, starting on page 140.

Ready? Then let's get started!

A

B

C

D

Psyduck uses Confusion . . . on itself!
Help it figure out which shadow is the exact match.

Help Cinderace complete these puzzles! In grids A and B below, fill the empty squares with the numbers 1 to 4. Each number can only appear once in each row, column, and 4x4 box.

A

2	4		
		2	
4			1
	3		

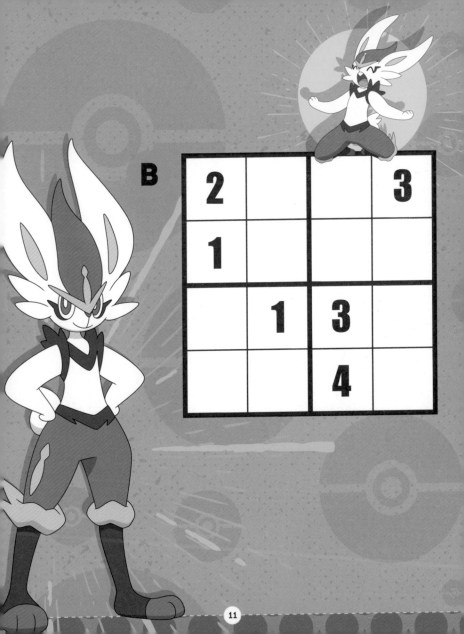

B

2			3
1			
	1	3	
		4	

ROW 1:

ROW 2:

ROW 3:

Draw the Pokémon that comes next in each row below.

Can you catch these Pokémon?
Find them in the word search!
Words go forward, backward, up,
down, and diagonal.

```
F J O G N W H W C B
E L H X E G I H Q W
E H T N A N A V C E
B G A C F R G Z A M
A O Z C I E K A F A
S F Z Z E C D X R C
U B A E K C E A F H
T R V U L P I X Y Q
D E H T I L W O R G
E O P K X R U L G H
```

14

CHARIZARD
EEVEE
FEEBAS
GENGAR
GROWLITHE
MEW
VULPIX

Help Eevee find Pikachu.

START

FINISH

MAZE

FINISH

START

Which piece on the left completes the picture on the right?

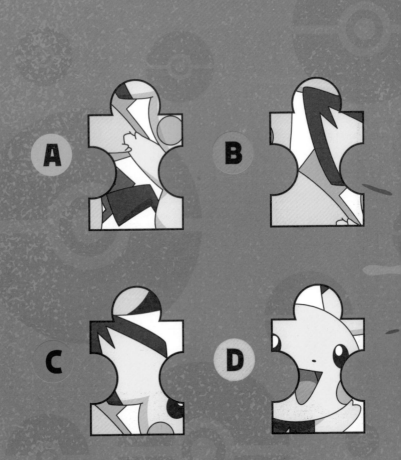

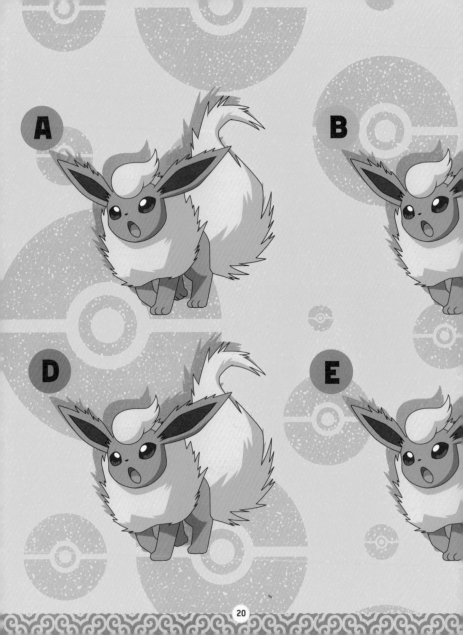

One picture of Flareon is different. Circle the odd one out.

DRAW DITTO

Can you copy the image of Ditto onto the grid on the right?

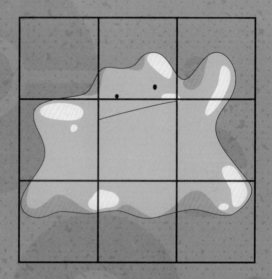

A

B

D

L

Crack the code to figure out the names of these Pokémon!

O	T	U	W

◯ ◯ ◯ ◯ ◯ ◯

List the words you can make out of the letters in . . .

GOTTA CATCH 'EM ALL!™

I CHOOSE YOU

Only two of these pictures of Butterfree are exactly the same. Can you find the matching pair?

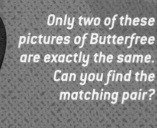

D

E

F

NOT LIKE THE OTHERS

Which of these is NOT a Fire-type Pokémon?
Circle your answer.

CINDERACE

CHARIZARD

VULPIX

GROWLITHE

FLAREON

GALVANTULA

PIKACHU

BOLTUND

GRUBBIN

JOLTEON

PICHU

J	T	Z	K	H	X	I	P	I	C
C	I	O	N	I	E	D	I	B	Q
X	L	G	Y	X	K	L	K	Z	P
K	I	Q	G	I	M	P	A	U	O
J	Z	L	Y	L	S	N	C	M	H
V	Y	G	E	Y	Y	U	H	Q	C
R	Y	U	D	E	H	P	U	X	A
F	X	U	W	D	T	P	U	L	M
D	C	I	D	X	J	S	G	F	S
K	S	N	O	R	L	A	X	G	F

Can you catch these Pokémon? Find them in the word search! Words go forward, backward, up, down, and diagonal.

JIGGLYPUFF
PIKACHU
PSYDUCK
SNORLAX

STEELIX
MACHOP
DEINO

33

THUNDER MAZE

Help Pichu through the maze to find Pikachu.

START

FINISH

PICHU
Tiny Mouse Pokémon

Type: Electric
Height: 1'00"
Weight: 4.4 lbs.

PIKACHU
Mouse Pokémon

Type: Electric
Height: 1'04"
Weight: 13.2 lbs.

1 Would you rather have Grookey, Sobble, or Scorbunny as your Pokémon partner? _____

Why? _____

_____

_____

_____

_____

2 Would you rather your Eevee evolve into Sylveon or Leafeon? _____

Why? _____

_____

_____

_____

3 Would you rather battle Steelix or Gyarados? _____

Why? _____

_____

_____

_____

_____

4 Would you rather try to catch Pokémon in a cave or in the sea? _____

Why? _____

_____

_____

_____

_____

WOULD YOU RATHER...

Bulbasaur is using Vine Whip to get the Grass-type icon. Which vine will get him there?

Follow the paths from each letter to discover the name of this Bite Pokémon!

Help Sobble count the water drops!
Write your answer below.

THERE ARE ⬤ DROPS

Use the code to help you discover what region these Pokémon come from.

WORD SEARCH

Can you catch these Pokémon? Find them in the word search! Words go forward, backward, up, down, and diagonal.

ALCREMIE

ARCANINE

BUTTERFREE

CORVIKNIGHT

DREDNAW

GENGAR

GROOKEY

GROWLITHE

LAPRAS

LUCARIO

MEOWSTIC

NICKIT

ONIX

RABOOT

RUFFLET

SCORBUNNY

SOBBLE

VULPIX

ZACIAN

ZAMAZENTA

```
C J E T W Y W V G C B S D R K
O R C O E W N R U U N S B S A
R A R P N L O N T L E U A K T
V B X Z M O F T U I P R S N N
I O E I K E E F M B P I I M E
K O B E N R O E U A R C X P Z
N T Y J F O R W L R K O K B A
I O I R A C U L S I U T C W M
G H E R L J U C T T U C D S A
H E N A I C A Z R K I C R R Z
T E H T I L W O R G T C E A L
A R C A N I N E K R W Y D G S
M J X L K I T W S B H R N N J
S O B B L E C D G E B E A E N
Q G C O J R L A Q G X I W G E
```

List the words you can make out of the letters in . . .

GARDEVOIR

Espurr used Confusion! Which picture exactly matches the Espurr on the top?

CONFUSION!

A

B

C

D

E

F

There are five differences between Picture A and Picture B. Can you find them? Circle each one.

PICTURE **A**

Come up with funny captions for each of these images!

Scorbunny is ready to battle! Who will you choose to challenge it? Draw the battle scene!

List your top five go-to Pokémon in a one-on-one battle against Scorbunny:

1. _____

2. _____

3. _____

4. _____

5. _____

SCORBUNNY
Rabbit Pokémon

- - - - - - - - - - - - - - - -

Type: Fire
Height: 1'0"
Weight: 9.9 lbs.

NORMAL

 GRASS

 GHOST

 WATER

 GROUND

 ICE

 PSYCHIC

SILICOBRA

GLACEON

THWACKEY

Can you identify the type of each of these Pokémon?
Draw a line between the Pokémon and its type symbol.

SKWOVET

ESPURR

DUSKULL

ARROKUDA

MAZE

Help Sobble find Grookey and Scorbunny!

START

FINISH

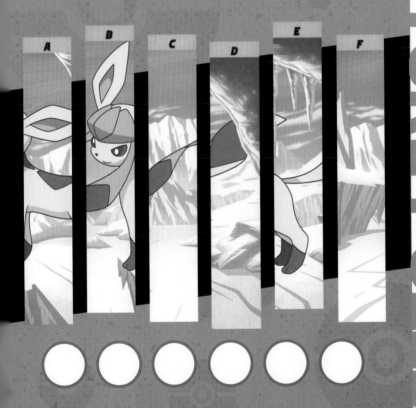

A   B   C   D   E   F

PICTURE PUZZLER

1

Grookey

?

Sobble

2

Pikachu

Pikachu

Pikachu

3

Bulbasaur

Ivysaur

?

Check out these Pokémon patterns! Write the name of the Pokémon who should come next in each row. You could even try drawing them!

Grookey   **Scorbunny**   **Sobble**

Psyduck   **Psyduck**

Bulbasaur   **Ivysaur**   **Venusaur**

Match the Pokémon to its shadow!

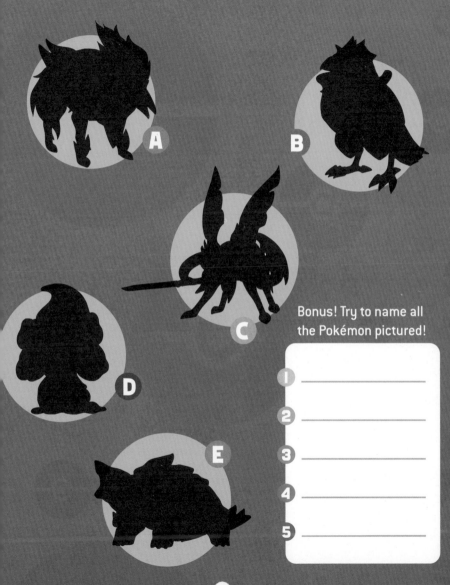

Bonus! Try to name all the Pokémon pictured!

1 _____

2 _____

3 _____

4 _____

5 _____

Which path connects Pancham to the Fighting-type icon?

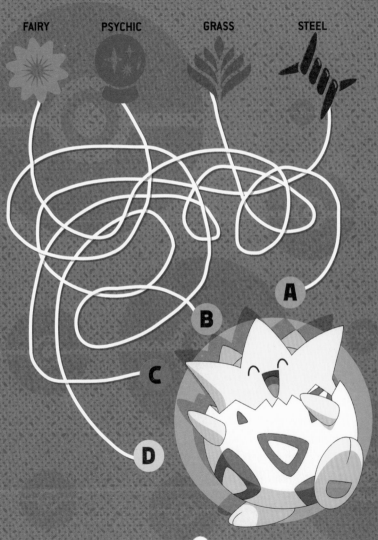

Which path connects Togepi to the Fairy-type icon?

FAIRY PSYCHIC GRASS STEEL

A

B

C

D

PICK A PATH

Each group has one Pokémon who doesn't fit with the others.
Can you spot them all? Circle the odd ones out.

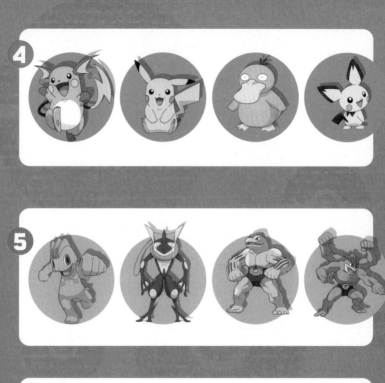

```
N Q N Z P E B V M S X F
F O O F K Z S A I W B V
K I E B Y Y D P M O S G
D U F T Q X D O E X G L
K R A N L H K R E O F K
J H E V I O G E E X N G
I V L P D W J O V W W S
P T F R O L F N E T P O
N K C V K L N V E V X O
K G T E A O L U E W V O
L W R R E R F I J P P W
W C E V R L D R Z J Z N
O O L R U M B R E O N C
N Y N O E C A L G E Y T
S F W S B U A Y H N X I
```

Can you catch Eevee and all of its known Evolutions?
Find them in the word search! Words go forward,
backward, up, down, and diagonal.

EEVEE

ESPEON

FLAREON

GLACEON

JOLTEON

LEAFEON

SYLVEON

UMBREON

VAPOREON

Check out these Pokémon patterns! Write the name of the Pokémon who should come next in each row. You could even try drawing them!

1
Eevee Espeon Flareon

2
Jigglypuff Togepi Jigglypuff

3
Yamper Yamper

Eeevee

?

Flareon

Togepi

Jigglypuff

?

Yamper

Yamper

Wooloo

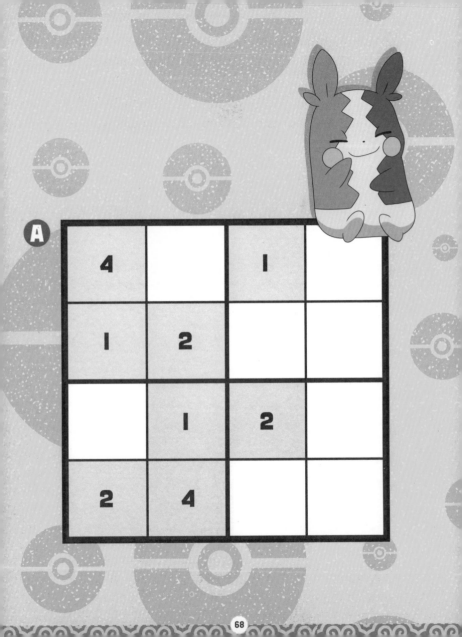

A

4		1	
1	2		
	1	2	
2	4		

68

Help Morpeko complete these puzzles!
In grids A and B below, fill the empty squares
with the numbers 1 to 4. Each number can only
appear once in each row, column, and 4x4 box.

B

		1	
	1		
4		3	1
1	3	2	

MINI SUDOKU

One picture of Zweilous is different. Circle the odd one out.

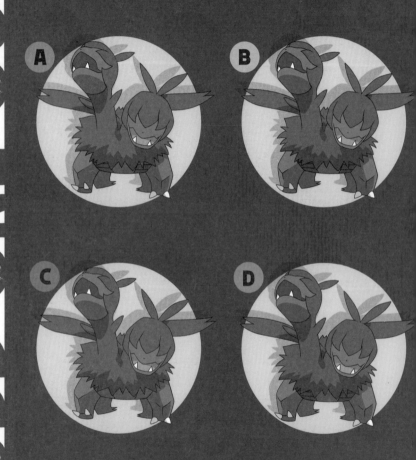

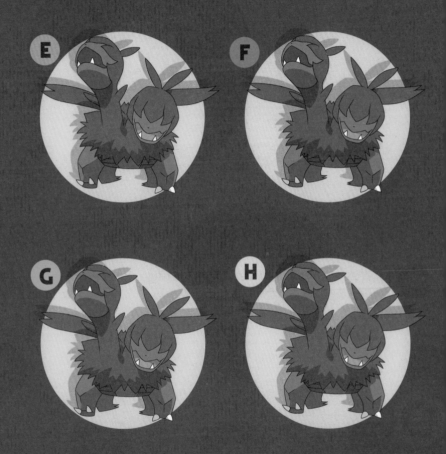

1 Would you rather have Yamper or Growlithe as your Pokémon partner? _____

Why? _____
_____
_____
_____
_____

2 Would you rather battle Rhyperior or Tyranitar?

_____

Why? _____
_____
_____
_____

3 Would you rather have your Eevee evolve into Jolteon or Flareon? _____

Why? _____

_____

_____

_____

4 Would you rather try to catch Pokémon at the beach or in the mountains? _____

Why? _____

_____

_____

_____

PUZZLE PIECES

Which piece on the left completes the picture on the right?

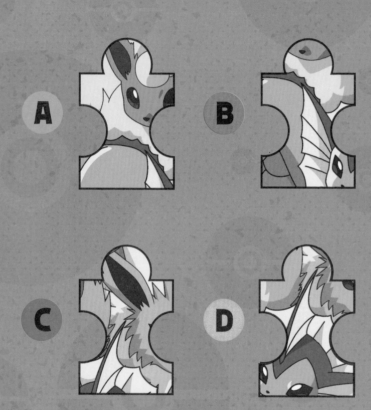

U S R P

Crack the code to figure out the names of these two Pokémon!

O

N

E

DRAW GENGAR

Can you copy the image of Gengar onto the grid on the right?

YAMPER
Puppy Pokémon

Type: Electric
Height: 1' 00"
Weight: 29.8 lbs.

Yamper is so excited! Help it figure out which shadow is its exact match.

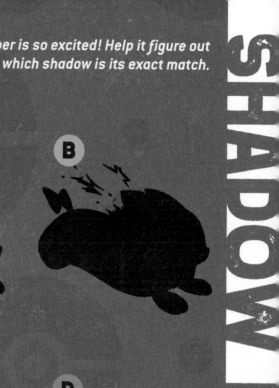

List the words you can make out of the letters in . . .

CHARMANDER

SCORBUNNY

Come up with funny captions for each of these images!

MATCHING LINEUP

These three rows of Pokémon should be identical. Write the correct letters in the blank spaces to complete each row.

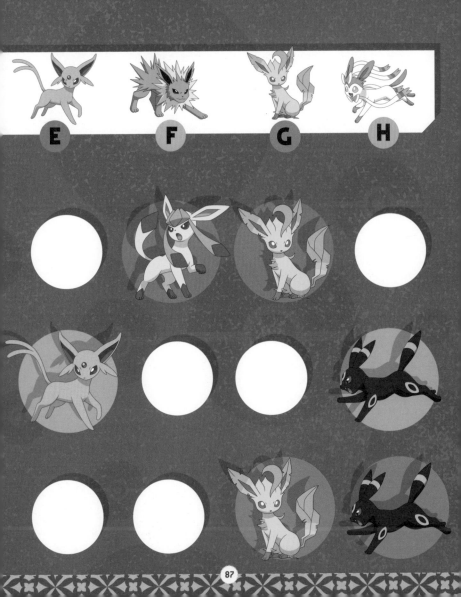

E   F   G   H

There are five differences between Picture A and Picture B. Can you find them? Circle each one.

Corviknight is ready to battle! Who will you choose to challenge it? Draw the battle scene!

List your top five go-to Pokémon in a one-on-one battle against Corviknight:

1. _____
2. _____
3. _____
4. _____
5. _____

CORVIKNIGHT
Raven Pokémon

Type: Flying-Steel
Height: 7'03"
Weight: 165.3 lbs.

TYRANITAR
Armor Pokémon

- - - - - - - - - - - - - - -

Type: Rock-Dark
Height: 6'07"
Weight: 445.3 lbs.

Roar! Help Tyranitar figure out which shadow is the exact match.

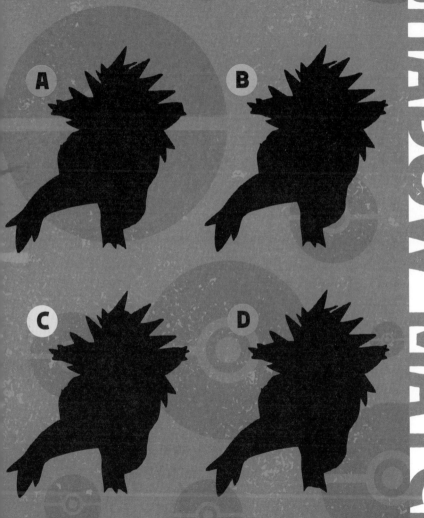

MINI SUDOKU

Help the Indeedee complete these puzzles! In grids A and B below, fill the empty squares with the numbers 1 to 4. Each number can only appear once in each row, column, and 4x4 box.

A

2			
3			1
		1	
1			2

B

1		2	
	2		1
	1	4	
3		1	

What's the name of this Fairy-type Pokémon? Cross out all the numbers from 1 to 9, then write the remaining letters in the white space and read the name.

5 9 8 Z 2 4 I 7 A 7 C I 3 9 5 I 4 2 A 3 2 8 N 4 5 I I

◯ ◯ ◯ ◯ ◯ ◯

Each of the four small pictures of Zamazenta has a different mistake in it. Find and circle all of them.

POKÉ BALL MAZE

Before you use these Poké Balls, can you find your way to the center of them?

START

START

FEEBAS

GENGAR

JIGGLYPUFF

GRENINJA

DEINO

CORVIKNIGHT

GYARADOS

CHARJABUG

EEVEE

Match the Pokémon categories with the correct Pokémon pictures by writing the right numbers inside the circles. The sum of the numbers in each row and column must be 15.

Raven Pokémon

Atrocious Pokémon

Shadow Pokémon

Fish Pokémon

Irate Pokémon

Evolution Pokémon

Battery Pokémon

Balloon Pokémon

Ninja Pokémon

POKEMON PATTERNS

Complete the sequences with the right numbers!

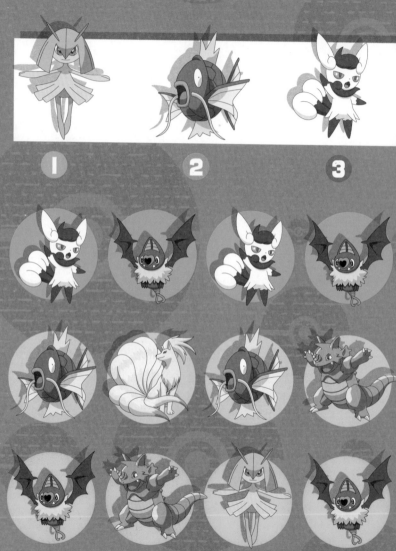

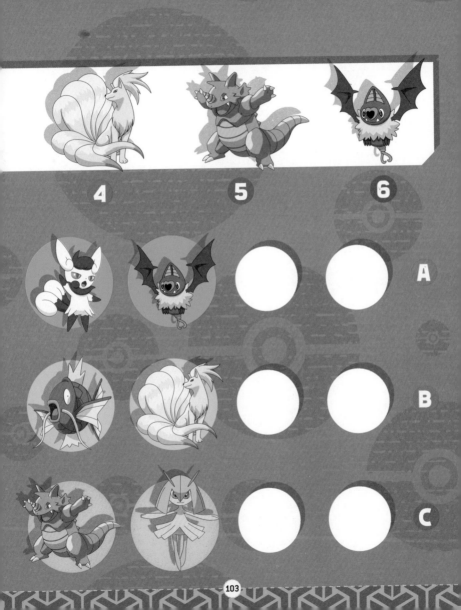

FAIRY

FIRE

FIGHTING

NORMAL

WATER

ELECTRIC

PSYCHIC

MACHOP

SNORLAX

LAPRAS

Can you identify the type of each of these Pokémon?
Draw a line between each Pokémon and its type symbol.

ALCREMIE

YAMPER

MEOWSTIC

ARCANINE

One picture of Togepi is different. Circle the odd one out.

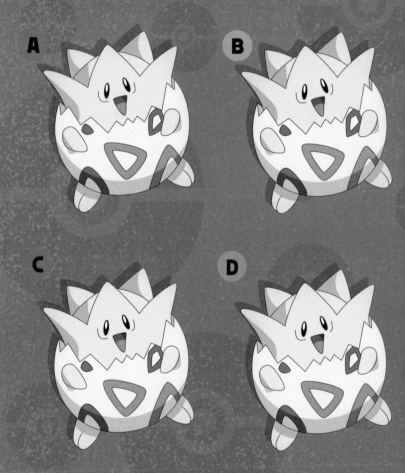

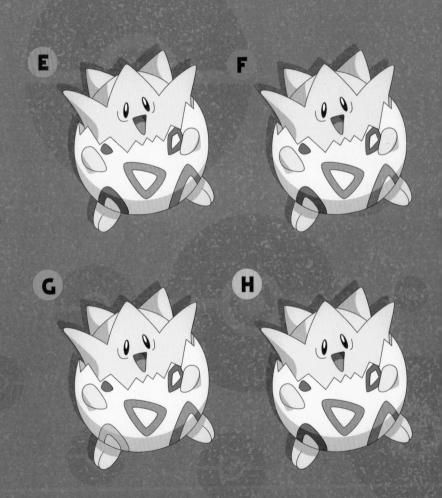

MAZE

Help Charmander find Bulbasaur and Squirtle!

START

FINISH

Leafeon is feeling all mixed up! Rearrange the letters to complete the picture.

WOULD YOU RATHER...

1 Would you rather have Pikachu or Scorbunny as your Pokémon partner? _____

Why? _____

_____

_____

_____

_____

2 Would you rather battle Blastoise, Venusaur, or Charizard? _____

_____

Why? _____

_____

_____

3 Would you rather have your Eevee evolve into Umbreon or Vaporeon? _____

Why? _____

_____

_____

_____

_____

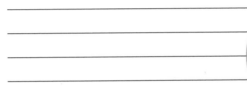

4 Would you rather try to catch Pokémon in the forest or in the grassland? _____

Why? _____

_____

_____

_____

_____

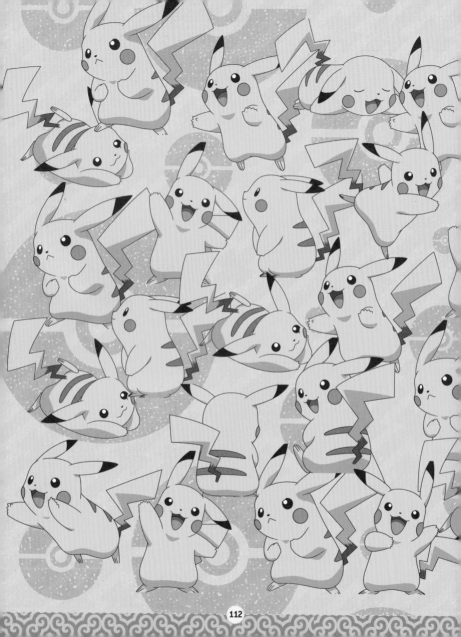

How many Pikachu can you find in this picture?

Match the Pokémon to its shadow!

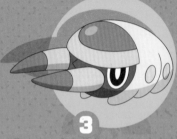

Bonus! Try to name all the Pokémon pictured!

1 _____
2 _____
3 _____
4 _____
5 _____

115

C	H	I
P	S	Y

CODE BREAKER

They are all

◯ ◯ ◯ ◯ ◯ ◯ ◯

— — — — — — —

-type Pokémon.

Find all the Pokémon pairs! There's only one without a match. Can you catch it? Write the letter and number of the spot in the grid below with the only lone Pokémon. (For example, one Pikachu is in A1).

	A	B
1		
2		
3		
4		
5		

C	D	E

W	O	O	L	O	O	K	U	E	H
S	O	O	L	O	O	W	J	B	M
V	W	O	O	L	O	O	O	M	R
D	W	B	O	M	B	O	S	X	T
F	O	W	O	O	L	O	O	C	T
A	O	L	V	O	L	U	B	A	C
Q	L	O	O	L	O	O	W	N	G
B	O	W	S	F	F	B	O	K	W
Q	O	O	B	J	I	M	L	W	H
C	T	G	U	L	J	P	K	V	O

Wooloo lives in herds. How many Wooloo can you find in this word search? They can be found going forward, backward, up, down, and diagonally. Circle them and then write the number you found below.

Wooloo in this puzzle

121

MATCHING LINEUP

These three rows of Pokémon should be identical. Write the correct letters in the blank spaces to complete each row.

A   B   C   D

122

Help Eevee find Vaporeon, Flareon, and Jolteon!

START

FINISH

START

FINISH

NAME THAT POKÉMON

What's the name of this Dark- and Ice-type Pokémon? Cross out all the numbers from 1 to 9, then write the remaining letters in the white space and read the name.

9 9 5 S 4 2 N I 8 7 E 5 2 A 3 3 I 6 S 4 7 8 E 4 9 L I 5 3

Each of the four small pictures of Weavile has a different mistake in it. Find and circle all of them.

Come up with funny captions for each of these images!

One picture of Gyarados is different. Circle the odd one out.

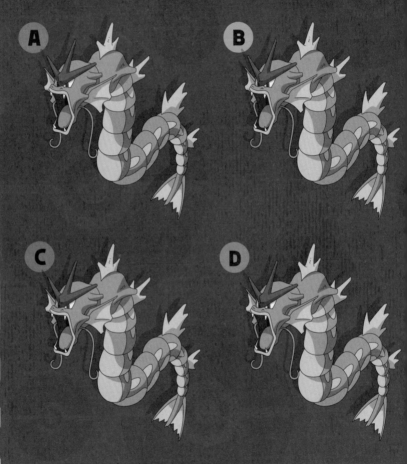

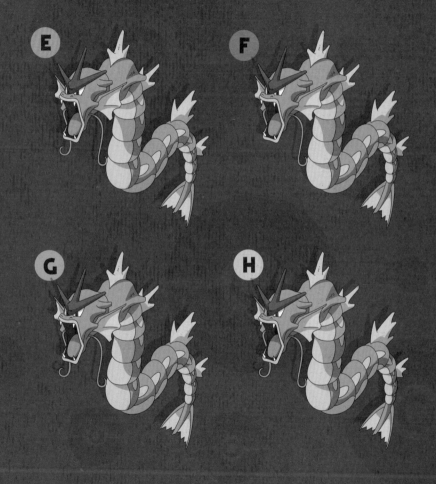

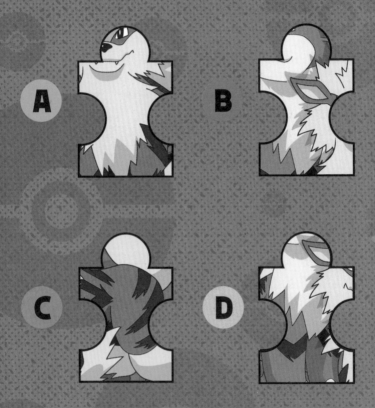

Which piece on the left completes the picture on the right?

PUZZLE PIECES

Help Hawlucha complete these puzzles! In grids A and B below, fill the empty squares with the numbers 1 to 4. Each number can only appear once in each row, column, and 4x4 box.

A

	1		3
4		2	
		3	
			2

B

1	3	2	4
		1	3
3		4	2
	4		1

135

List the words you can make out of the letters in . . .

BLASTOISE

VAPOREON

Greninja is ready to battle! Who will you choose to challenge it? Draw the battle scene!

List your top five go-to Pokémon in a one-on-one battle against Greninja:

1. _____

2. _____

3. _____

4. _____

5. _____

GRENINJA
Ninja Pokémon

Type: Water-Dark
Height: 4'11"
Weight: 88.2 lbs.

PAGE 4–5:
B is the correct path

PAGE 6–7:

Pikachu – Electric
Grookey – Grass
Scorbunny – Fire
Sobble – Water
Eevee – Normal
Grubbin – Bug
Pancham – Fighting

PAGE 8–9:

A is the exact match

PAGE 10–11:

A

2	4	1	3
3	1	2	4
4	2	3	1
1	3	4	2

B

2	4	1	3
1	3	2	4
4	1	3	2
3	2	4	1

PAGE 12–13:

ROW 1:

ROW 2:

ROW 3:

PAGE 14–15:

F	J	O	G	N	W	H	W	C	B
E	L	H	X	E	G	I	H	Q	M
E	H	T	N	A	N	A	V	C	E
B	G	A	C	F	R	G	Z	A	W
A	O	Z	C	I	E	K	A	F	A
S	F	Z	Z	E	C	D	X	R	C
U	B	A	E	K	C	E	A	F	H
T	R	V	U	L	P	I	X	Y	Q
D	E	H	T	I	L	W	O	R	G
E	O	P	K	X	R	U	L	G	H

PAGE 16–17:

PAGE 18–19:

A

PAGE 20–21:

D

PAGE 24–25:

DUBWOOL and WOOBAT

PAGE 26:

Some words include: CALL, COAT, GATE, GOAL, GOAT, MATCH, MATE, TALL, TEACH, TELL

PAGE 27:

Some words include: OUCH, HOUSE, HOSE, SHOE, ICES, ICY, HIS, YES, SHY, COO

PAGE 28–29:

C and F are the matching pair

PAGE 30:

Galvantula

PAGE 31:

Grubbin

PAGE 32-33:

PAGE 34–35:

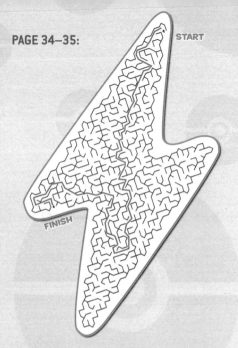

START

FINISH

PAGE 38:

B

PAGE 39:

DREDNAW

PAGE 40:

There are 16 drops.

PAGE 41:

GALAR

PAGE 42–43:

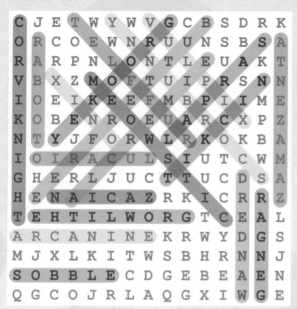

PAGE 44:

Some words include: AIR, DARE, DIVER, EAR, GEAR, GIVE, ODE, OVER, REAR, VIDEO

PAGE 45:

E

PAGE 46–47:

PAGE 52–53:

Silicobra – Ground
Thwackey – Grass
Skwovet – Normal
Arrokuda – Water
Espurr – Psychic
Duskull – Ghost
Glaceon – Ice

PAGE 54:

PAGE 55:

PAGE 56–57:

1: Scorbunny
2: Psyduck
3: Venusaur

PAGE 58–59:

1-B, 2-D, 3-E, 4-C, 5-A

Bonus: 1-Corviknight, 2-Alcremie, 3-Drednaw, 4-Zacian, 5-Zamazenta

PAGE 60:

B

PAGE 61:

A

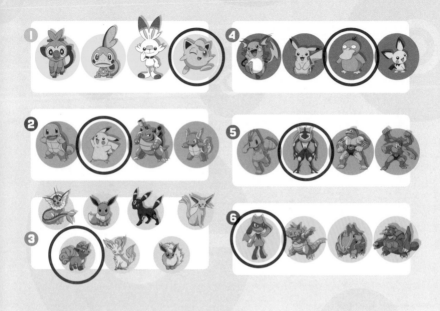

```
N Q N Z P E B V M S X F
F O O F K Z S A I W B V
K I E B Y Y D P M O S G
D U F T Q X D O E X G L
K R A N L H K R E O F K
J H E V I O G E E X N G
I V L P D W J O V W W S
P T F R O L F N E T P O
N K C V K L N V E V X O
K G T E A O L U E W V O
L W R R E R F I J P P W
W C E V R L D R Z J Z N
O O L R U M B R E O N C
N Y N O E C A L G E Y T
S F W S B U A Y H N X I
```

148

PAGE 66–67:

1: Espeon
2: Togepi
3: Wooloo

PAGE 68–69:

A

4	3	1	2
1	2	4	3
3	1	2	4
2	4	3	1

B

3	4	1	2
2	1	4	3
4	2	3	1
1	3	2	4

PAGE 70–71:

C is the odd one out.

PAGE 74–75:

D

PAGE 76–77:

ESPURR and ESPEON

PAGE 80–81:

C is the exact match

PAGE 82:

Some words include: MARCHED, RANCH, ERRAND, ARCADE, AHEAD, NAME, CRANE, CARE, DEAR, HEAD, HAND, NERD, READ

PAGE 83:

Some words include: BOUNCY, RUNNY, SUNNY, NOUN, BORN, YOURS, BUSY, NOSY, CORN, RUBY, SNOB, RUN, BUS, YOU

PAGE 86–87:

PAGE 88–89:

PAGE 92–93:

B is the exact match.

PAGE 94–95:

2	1	3	4
3	4	2	1
4	2	1	3
1	3	4	2

A

1	3	2	3
4	2	4	1
2	1	4	3
3	4	1	2

B

PAGE 96:

ZACIAN

PAGE 97:

PAGE 98:

PAGE 99:

PAGE 100–101:

4 FEEBAS

3 GENGAR

8 JIGGLYPUFF

9 GRENINJA

5 DEINO

1 CORVIKNIGHT

2 GYARADOS

7 CHARJABUG

6 EEVEE

102–103:

A: 3, 6
B: 2, 4
C: 6, 5

PAGE 104–105:

Machop – Fighting
Meowstic – Psychic
Snorlax – Normal
Lapras – Water
Alcremie – Fairy
Arcanine – Fire
Yamper – Electric

PAGE 106–107:

G is the odd one out.

PAGE 108:

PAGE 112–113:

37 Pikachu

PAGE 114–115:

1-D, 2-A, 3-E, 4-B, 5-C

Bonus:
1-Gastly, 2-Flapple, 3-Grubbin, 4-Arcanine, 5-Joltik

PAGE 116–117:

PSYCHIC

PAGE 118–119:

4B.
Bonus: Haunter

PAGE 120–121:

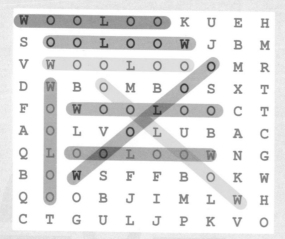

8 Wooloo in this puzzle

PAGE 122–123:

PAGE 124:

PAGE 125:

PAGE 126:

SNEASEL

PAGE 127:

F is the odd one out.

B

2	1	4	3
4	3	2	1
1	2	3	4
3	4	1	2

A

1	3	2	4
4	2	1	3
3	1	4	2
2	4	3	1

B

136:

Some words include: STABLE, BOAST, BLOAT, BEAST, STEAL, TABLE, STALE, BOLT, SAIL, LOSE, BASE, SEA

137:

Some words include: APRON, OPERA, PROVE, RAVEN, EARN, OPEN, NOPE, OVEN, PANE, POOR, OAR, RAN